MORE EASY
RECORDER
TUNES

Anya Suschitzky

Designed and illustrated by Simone Abel

Edited by Anthony Marks

Original music and arrangements by Anya Suschitzky

Music engraving by Poco Ltd, Letchworth, Herts

This book has lots of tunes for you to play on your descant recorder. As you go through the book, the tunes get more difficult and may need more practice. You might also find some notes you have not played before.

In the section called "Music help" on page 62, there is a fingering chart which shows you how to play all the notes in the book. There are hints on playing and performing, and the Italian words and music directions used in the book are also explained on page 62.

Throughout the book there are lots of facts about composers and their music, and hints on recorder technique. Near the end there are some duets for two descant recorders, and pieces for recorder and piano.

Michael Finnegan

The Banjo

Up-beats

Not all pieces begin on the first beat of the bar. Some begin on the last beat, which is called the up-beat or anacrusis. If there is an up-beat, the last bar of the piece will be incomplete. When you add the two part bars together they make one full bar.

Three rounds

The tunes on this page are rounds. They can be played as solos, or by more than one person. When several people play, each one starts a few bars apart, as shown by the numbers in boxes.

When the first player gets to the number 2, the second player starts at the beginning. When the first player gets to the number 3 the third player starts, and so on.

Hymn tune

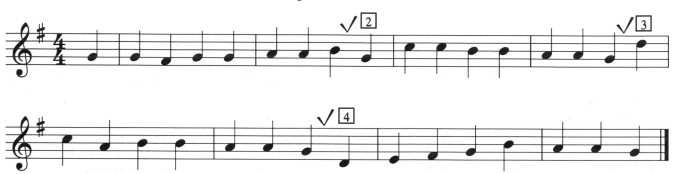

Can you hear?

The cuckoo

6

Canon

A canon is another name for a round (see page 6). You can play canons and rounds several times over.

This tune is by a composer called Praetorius (c.1571-1621).

Old Abra'm Brown

When you play with friends, listen to them carefully so that you all stay in time.

Farewell

The F sharp in this round is called an accidental. It is written on the stave because it is not in the key signature.

You can find out more about accidentals on page 12.

Greek air

Row, row, row your boat

Here is another round. It has three eighth note beats in each bar.

The recorder king

King Henry VIII of England (1491-1547) owned 76 recorders. Some were made of oak, silver or ivory. He kept families of different sized recorders in big cases together.

Henry VIII wrote lots of music.

Playing high G

Fanfare

A fanfare is a short piece for trumpets. Fanfares are played to celebrate important people or events.

At the bottom of the page you can find out what *moderato* means. There are also hints on how to play high A.

Playing high A

You have to blow quite hard to play high notes.

Make sure you uncover the thumb hole properly, or you will get low A.

Moderato means "moderately fast". (There is a list of Italian terms on page 62.)

10

German song

Theme from Symphony no.5

Schubert wrote many famous songs. You will find some of these on pages 31, 38, and 44.

The dog and the cat

Accidentals

A sharp, flat or natural that is not in the key signature is called an accidental. Accidentals are written before the note they change. An accidental applies until the end of the bar, after which you go back to the original key signature.

Hungarian national anthem

Sharps and flats

Have you noticed that you use the same fingering for G sharp and A flat? This is because they are different names for the same note, which is halfway between G and A. The same applies to the other sharps and flats. C sharp is the same as D flat (the note halfway between C and D), and B flat is the same as A sharp (halfway between A and B).

Minuet

This piece is by the German composer Bach, (1685-1750). It comes from a book of tunes that he wrote for his wife, Anna Magdalena.

The minuet is a French dance. It was very popular in the 17th century. Minuets are in $\frac{3}{4}$ time and not too fast.

Dynamics

The tune on this page has signs which tell you how loud to play. They are called dynamics.

This means *forte*, or "loud".

This is a crescendo. *Crescendo* means "get louder".

This means *piano*, or "soft".

This is a diminuendo. *Diminuendo* means "get softer".

Emphasizing notes

A line above or below a note is called a tenuto. It tells you to lengthen the note to make it sound more important.

In this piece, try making the other two beats in the bar a little bit shorter. This would make it sound like a dance.

Many tunes do not tell you which notes to emphasize. They let you decide how you want the piece to sound.

Sarabande

This piece is by the Italian composer Corelli (1653-1713). A sarabande is a Spanish dance in which the second beat of the bar is emphasized.

mf is short for *mezzo forte*, which means "quite loud". You can find out what *largo* and *rit.* mean below.

This tune is by the English composer Campion (1567-1620)

Jack and Jone

Breathing

When you play slowly you need to take big breaths.

Try not to lift your shoulders.

The best way to fill your lungs is to breathe from your tummy upward.

Keep your throat and mouth relaxed, as you do when you sigh.

Largo

Largo means "slow and stately".

Rit. means "slow down".

Buy a broom

Recorder facts

Recorders are made of wood or plastic, and come in different sizes. The most common are the sopranino, descant, treble, tenor, and bass.

In the 16th century, there were at least eleven sizes. Books written at that time tell us that early recorders could be played with either the right or the left hand on top. These recorders were developed from whistles which had only four holes and were made from horn or bone.

Deck the halls

The time signature of this tune means there are two half note beats in each bar.

O Christmas tree

18

The soldier's march

Trampoline jelly bean

Now I see

Come fill, my good fellow

The last rose of summer

21

Theme from Beethoven's Violin Concerto

A concerto is a piece for a solo instrument and an orchestra.

Theme from a string quartet by Haydn

This string quartet is by Haydn (1739-1809). Haydn was one of the first composers to write string quartets.

A string quartet is a piece for two violins, one viola, and one cello.

Old French song

23

Minuet

Minuetto allegretto

The duckling in the meadow

Moderato

24

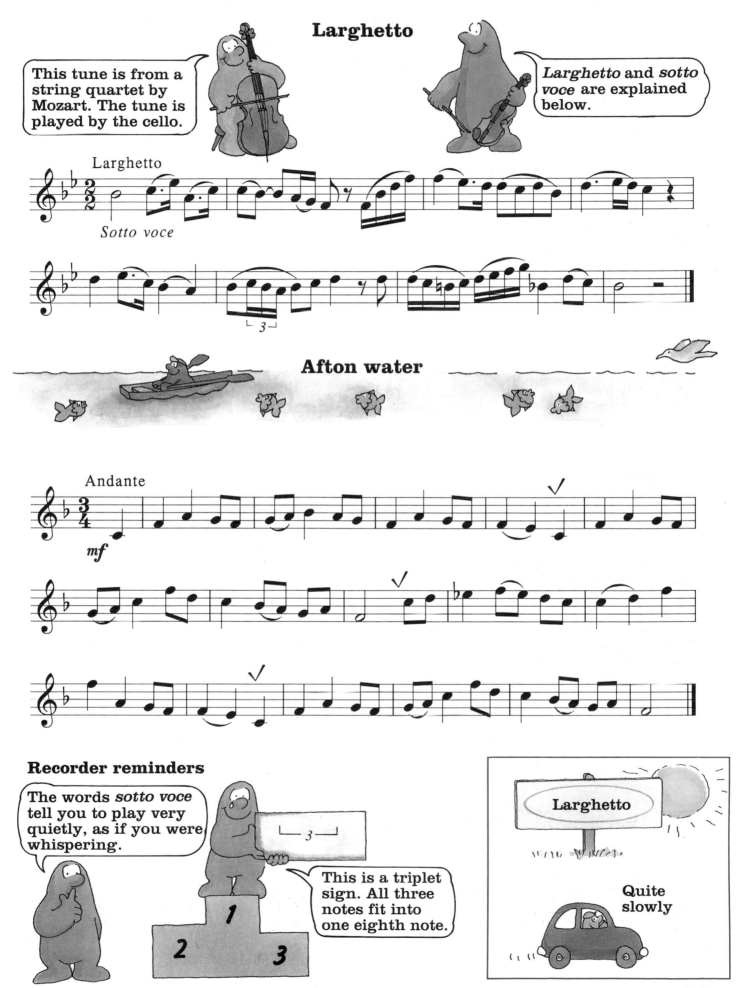

Theme from String Sextet no.1 by Brahms

This tune is by the German composer Brahms (1833-1897). A string sextet is for two violins, two violas, and two cellos.

Poco allegretto e grazioso means "quite fast and gracefully".

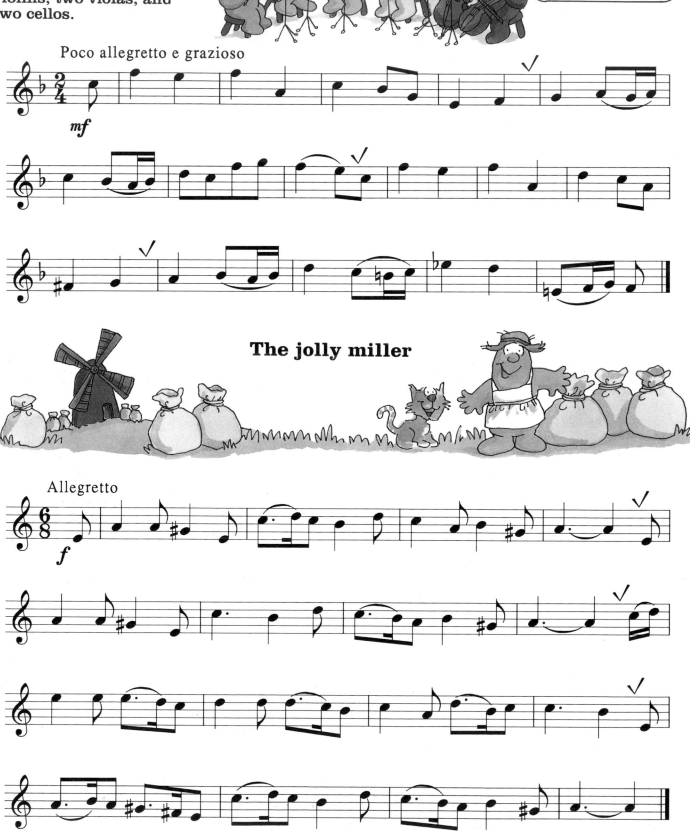

The jolly miller

O come, o come, Emmanuel

The time signature of this tune changes because there are extra beats in the last phrase. Count quarter notes throughout.

Theme from the Hunt Quartet

This piece is by Mozart. It is called the *Hunt Quartet* because the beginning sounds like a hunting horn.

Dolce means "sweetly".

Vivace means "quickly and lively".

Trumpet tune

Tonguing

You can make your playing sound smooth or spiky by altering the way the tip of your tongue touches the mouthpiece of the recorder. This is called tonguing. Using different tonguings allows you to play the music in the style you like best.

Tonguing is like saying the beginnings of words. Different letters make different sounds on the recorder, just as they do when you speak. The most important letters for tonguing on the recorder are "t", "d" and "g".

German dance

Theme from Symphony no.5

Minuet

The tunes on this page are dances by Mozart. He wrote them for his opera *Don Giovanni*.

Although the tunes have different time signatures, Mozart managed to write them to be played together. You can play them as a duet if you like, but it is fairly difficult.

Contredanse

To play these dances together, start the minuet two beats before the contredanse, and play it without repeats. The contredanse player begins when the minuet player reaches the *.

When you play this duet the contredanse will finish a little after the end of the minuet.

30 * When the minuet player reaches this sign, the contredanse player begins.

Wandering

More about emphasizing notes

An accent is written above or below a note to show that it should be emphasized. When you see an accented note, play it a little louder than the other notes.

31

Scales and arpeggios

Scales are groups of notes which go up and down by step. There are many kinds of scale. The most common scale is the major scale. It is made of two kinds of step, small ones and large ones.

The smallest step between two notes is called a semitone (see page 14). The largest step in a major scale is called a tone. It is made of two small steps (semitones) put together.

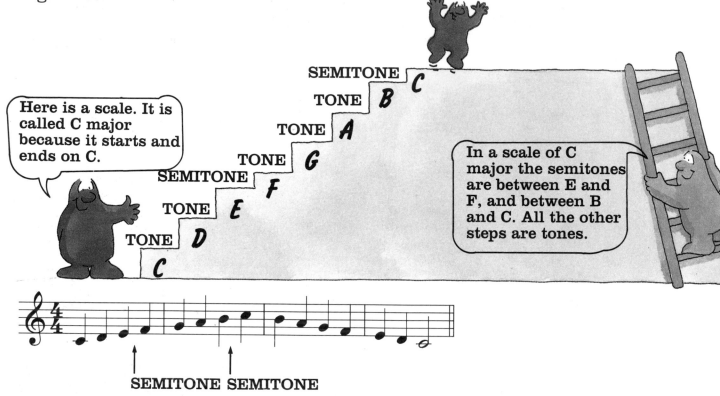

Here is a scale. It is called C major because it starts and ends on C.

In a scale of C major the semitones are between E and F, and between B and C. All the other steps are tones.

Arpeggios are groups of notes which pick out the important notes in a scale. The steps in arpeggios are larger than the steps in scales, but they are still made of different combinations of tones and semitones.

Here is an arpeggio. It is called C major, and contains the notes C, E and G.

The first two steps in this arpeggio are called thirds because you count up three notes between C and E and between E and G.

The last step is called a fourth because you count up four notes between G and C.

The Birdcatcher's song

This tune is from Mozart's opera The Magic Flute. The magic flute plays the demi-semiquaver* scales.

There are four demisemiquavers in one quaver beat.

The jelly walk

A *tempo* means "go back to the original speed".

* In North America, demisemiquavers are known as "thirty-second notes".

The happy farmer

This tune is from a book of pieces by Schumann, called *Album for the Young*.

Dal S al Fine means you go back to the sign and play until you reach the word *Fine*.

Allegretto

f

Fine

Dal S al Fine

This tune contains high and low D sharps.

Sad tune

Find out how to play both D sharps below.

Moderato

p

Playing low D sharp

Playing high D sharp

The best way to uncover the hole for low D sharp is to slide your finger a little to the right.

35

My old hen

Happy march

Coventry Carol

The last note of this tune is a B natural. This kind of ending is called a *tierce de picardie*.

Andante

Sir Watkyn's dream

This is a Welsh folk tune.

Allegretto

Polonaise

Rhine legend

This tune is by Mahler (1860-1911). It is from a group of songs called *The Youth's Magic Horn*.

The story of the Rhine is an ancient German legend about some magical women. They guard a hoard of gold at the bottom of the River Rhine.

This tune is by the Dutch composer Jacob van Eyck (1590-1657). He wrote lots of music for the renaissance recorder (see opposite).

Simon's tune

Compared with your recorder, renaissance recorders were wider inside. They were usually made from one piece of wood rather than three.

Poor little baby

We wish you a merry Christmas

Sarabande

This sarabande is by Corelli. It contains a high G sharp (see below).

Corelli was a very rich composer. He had a large collection of paintings in his palace.

Recorder composers

Corelli lived during a period of music history known as the Baroque era (1600-1750). Baroque composers wrote lots of sonatas which were usually in several movements. They were for a solo instrument (or sometimes two) and the harpsichord.

Composers who wrote sonatas for the recorder include Vivaldi (1678-1741), Handel (1685-1759), and Telemann (1681-1767). You can find recordings of their sonatas in a library or record shop.

Playing G sharp

Gavotte

This gavotte is by Bach. Bach wrote lots of gavottes and other dances which he put together in groups called suites.

Many of Bach's suites were for the harpsichord. They included other dances such as the allemande, the sarabande, the jig, and the courante.

Rain of tears

This is a song by Schubert. It comes from *The Fair Maid of the Mill*.

La Marseillaise

This tune is the French National Anthem.

The first rest counts as a dotted eighth note.

44

Theme from the Emperor Quartet

This theme is by Haydn. It is from his *Emperor Quartet*. It is also the German National Anthem.

Haydn wrote this tune for a series of variations. Variations are tunes based on a theme, but they change some of its notes, rhythms, or tempo.

Farandole

The farandole (a dance from southern France) is often played on a pipe and drum. *Allegro con brio* means "quickly and energetically".

Edinburgh town

This is a Scottish folk tune. The dotted rhythms in bars 4 and 15 are known as 'Scotch snaps'.

When you play Scotch snaps, try to put an accent on the first note of each pair.

Recorder concertos

Concertos written in the Baroque era sometimes have more than one solo instrument. They are called *concerti grossi*, which means "big concertos". Bach wrote six *concerti grossi* called the *Brandenburg Concertos*. In no.2 there are solos for a violin, a trumpet, an oboe and a recorder. In no.4 there are solos for a violin and two recorders.

Vivaldi wrote several recorder concertos, including some for the sopranino, the smallest recorder.

They are very difficult to play, but exciting to listen to.

The Fairy Queen

Gavotte

Trills

48

March

Slavonic dance

English dance

Bourrée

This tune is by Handel. It is from a piece called *Music for the Royal Fireworks*.

The bourrée is an old French dance. *Leggiero* means "lightly and delicately".

The merry wooing of Robin and Joan

The English composer Byrd (1543-1623) wrote variations on this tune for a big book of keyboard music called the *Fitzwilliam Virginal Book*.

You can find out more about variations below.

Recorder composers

Many composers in Byrd's time wrote sets of variations. Sometimes, each variation was harder than the last one. This was to allow performers to show how well they could play.

Composers often wrote simple tunes. They knew performers would decorate or ornament the music by adding trills and mordents as they went along.

The asterisks in the tune above show where the performer might have added trills or mordents.

Try playing the tune on this page as it is written. Then play it again, adding your own ornaments.

52

Minuet

Rigadoon

56

Sarabande

This duet is by the French composer Boismortier (1689-1755). It was written for flutes but like lots of flute music, it works well on the recorder too.

There are mordents in the second bar. Find out how to play them on page 49.

Hatikvah

This is an old Jewish melody. *Hatikvah* means "hope".

Welcome friends

This duet is a French-Canadian folk song.

Minuet

Gavotte

This gavotte is from a flute sonata by Handel.

Music help

This list explains the Italian terms used in the book.

allegretto – not too quickly
allegro – quickly
andante – at a walking pace
a tempo – in time
cantabile – singing
con espressione – with expression
con moto – with movement
crescendo – getting louder
Dal ％ al Fine – from the sign to *Fine*
D.C. al Fine – back to the beginning to *Fine*

diminuendo – getting softer
dolce – sweetly
fine – the end
forte (f) – loudly
grazioso – gracefully
larghetto – quite slowly
largo – slowly
legato – smoothly
leggiero – lightly
lento – slowly
maestoso – grandly
mezzo forte (mf) – quite loudly

moderato – at a moderate speed
molto – very
piano (p) – quietly
poco – a little
poco a poco – little by little
presto – very quickly
ritenuto (rit.) – held back
scherzando – playfully
sotto voce – very quietly
staccato – short
vivace – quickly and lively

Practising

Before you play a piece you don't know, it is a good idea to look through it. First try clapping the rhythms or singing the tune.

If there are any difficult bits, play them slowly, then gradually work up to the correct speed. You can also invent exercises for yourself. For instance, try playing the difficult bits with a new rhythm. When you go back to the right rhythm the music will seem easier.

Performing

Not every performance of a piece of music is the same. This is because everyone has their own ideas about how the music should sound.

Once you can play the right notes, you can make very small changes to the signs (dynamics, tempo and tonguings) in order to play the piece exactly as you want to. This is called interpretation. Interpretation is what gives your playing its own special character.

Fingering chart

This chart shows the fingerings for all the notes in the book.

| Note: | C | C#/D♭ | D | D#/E♭ | E | F | F#/G♭ | G | G#/A♭ | A | A#/B♭ | B | C' | C#/D♭' | D' | D#/E♭' | E' | F' | F#/G♭' | G' | G#/A♭' | A' | A#/B♭' | B' |

62

Index of tunes

Index